THE BOXCAR CHILDREN®

BOOK 151

CREATED BY
GERTRUDE
CHANDLER
WARNER

THE SEA TURTLE MYSTERY

THE BOXCAR CHILDREN MYSTERIES

THE BOXCAR CHILDREN ®

CREATED BY
GERTRUDE CHANDLER WARNER

BOOK
151

THE SEA TURTLE MYSTERY

ILLUSTRATED BY
ANTHONY VanARSDALE

ALBERT WHITMAN & COMPANY
CHICAGO, ILLINOIS

ISBN 978-0-8075-0753-7 (hardcover)
ISBN 978-0-8075-0746-9 (paperback)

Printed in the United States of America
10 9 8 7 6 5 4 3 2 1 LB 24 23 22 21 20 19

Illustrations by Anthony VanArsdale

Visit the Boxcar Children online at www.boxcarchildren.com.
For more information about Albert Whitman & Company,
visit our website at www.albertwhitman.com.

100 years of Albert Whitman & Company
Celebrate with us in 2019!

Contents

What's in the Water?

Six-year-old Benny Alden was confused. He tilted his head to the side and looked at the map in his sister Violet's hands. Violet was ten, and she was helping teach Benny how to read the map. The two were in the back seat of Grandfather's car on their way to a place called Padre Island. Benny pointed. "I know this word says *island*, but I thought islands were round. This one looks like a big line on the map."

"Padre Island is a barrier island," said Henry from the front seat. Henry was the oldest of the Alden children. At fourteen, he had learned about different land formations in school. "Most barrier islands are long and narrow and not very far from

1

land. They're kind of like big sandbars."

Benny's twelve-year-old sister Jessie spoke up next. "Look out the window! We're about to cross the bridge to the island!"

Within just a few minutes, Grandfather pulled into a parking lot and stopped the car. It had been a long journey. But the view was worth it.

Behind them, seagrasses and flowering vines covered the sand dunes. The beach and the ocean were right in front of them. The four children jumped out and ran down to the water. Grandfather followed with Watch, the Aldens' wirehaired terrier.

Violet couldn't believe what she saw. "There are millions and millions of shells here!" she said, picking up a couple. "All different kinds too." She was so excited about the shells she didn't even notice when a big blue heron flew overhead.

"It's such a wide-open space. We can see for miles," said Jessie. "I'm going to take lots of pictures."

"Where are all the buildings?" asked Benny.

"There aren't any houses or shops on this part of the island," said Grandfather. "This is a national

seashore, which is a lot like a national park. The land has been set aside so it can be protected."

Henry walked back toward the car to a sandy area in front of the dunes. "Jessie, don't you think this is a good place for the tent?" he asked. "It's close to the visitor center and the ranger station."

"Yes, it's perfect," said Jessie.

The children piled everything at the spot Henry had chosen. When they were finished and Grandfather was closing up the back of the car, a truck sped past them. It drove right off the road and onto the sand. Then it sped down the beach.

"I didn't know people could drive on the beach," said Henry. "That looks like fun."

"This seashore is very long," said Grandfather. "It would take a lot of time to travel all the way down it on foot. Vehicles help people get there faster. There are speed limits, but you'll have to watch out for cars on the beach."

"We will," said Jessie.

"Are you sure you don't want to camp with us, Grandfather?" Benny asked.

Grandfather smiled. "I'm sure. I'll be happy sitting

in a rocking chair on the porch of the inn back on the mainland. But when I see you in the evenings, you'll have to tell me all about your adventures."

The children promised they would, then said good-bye. After Grandfather had gone, the Aldens got to work setting up the tent and organizing the supplies. When they were done, Jessie looked over everything. She liked to keep things organized. "It looks like we have everything we need," she said.

"It's a lot more than we had when we lived in the boxcar," said Henry.

"That seems like such a long time ago," Violet said. "I can't believe we didn't even want to meet Grandfather back then."

After the Aldens' parents had died, the children had run away. They hadn't wanted to live with their grandfather because they were afraid he would be mean. They found an old boxcar in the woods and had lived in it until their grandfather found them. He turned out not to be mean at all! Now they lived with Grandfather back in Greenfield, Connecticut, and the boxcar was their clubhouse.

Jessie picked up her camera and put the strap

around her neck. "It was nice of Grandfather to arrange this vacation for us. I don't know about everyone else, but I'm ready to explore the beach."

"Yay!" Benny yelled, running down to the ocean. "The water is so warm!" he called to the others. He jumped up and down, splashing. Then all of a sudden he stopped and looked down. Then he looked back up at the others. Jessie could see that he was scared as he ran back to the beach.

"There's something in there!" he yelled. "It's after me!"

"Whoa, Benny, don't be scared," Henry said. "The water is too shallow for a big fish."

Jessie waded in and looked down at the water. "Sometimes the way the waves move over the sand makes it look like something is moving in the water. It's just a trick on your eyes."

"But I did see something," Benny said. He stretched his arms out as wide as he could. "Something this big."

Henry and Watch came to the edge of the water as a big wave came in and then rolled back. Watch barked and stepped back a few steps.

What's in the Water?

"There!" yelled Benny.

Where Benny pointed, a big clump of sand seemed to rise up from the sandy bottom. Watch barked again at the strange shape. Then another wave washed some of the sand away, revealing a strange-looking creature. Benny was right. There was something in the shallows. Something big!

Not a Bird's Nest

"A giant sea turtle!" said Violet. The turtle was much bigger than any she had seen. It had a smooth, light gray shell and long flipper arms, which it was using to pull itself up onto the beach.

"It's moving so slow," said Benny. "Even for a turtle. Is it sick?"

"I think it's moving so slowly because it doesn't have legs like a land turtle," Jessie said. "I've seen these kinds of turtles on TV. It's amazing how they use their flippers to glide through the water and ride the currents."

"Should we help it?" Violet asked. "I think it's confused."

"Silly turtle. Go back to the water," Benny called.

"Even if it is confused, we can't pick it up," Henry said. "It's too big."

As they watched the turtle crawl up the sand, they heard a voice call, "Don't go any closer! Stay back! Stay back!"

Violet jumped. She hadn't noticed anyone nearby, but a man got out of a white van near the dunes and ran toward them waving his arms. "Stay away! Keep your dog away!"

The man sounded upset, and the Aldens stepped back.

"We weren't going to hurt it," Henry told him. "We were just wondering why it was out of the water."

The man glared at them. "This whole area is a sea turtle nesting ground. This particular species is endangered, so we have to protect them as best we can."

"What does endangered mean?" Benny asked.

"It means there aren't many of them still living in the wild," the man said.

"Are you a park ranger?" Violet asked him. The man wasn't wearing a uniform, but he wasn't wearing normal beach clothes either, except for a big straw hat. His tan pants and white shirt looked like the clothes Grandfather wore to his office in the summer.

"No, I'm not a ranger, but I am a turtle expert." The man motioned at the beach. "You should go play somewhere else."

"So this turtle is going to its nest?" asked Violet. She didn't see anything that looked like a nest.

"It digs a hole in the sand," the man said. "That is its nest."

Just as the man said this, the turtle stopped crawling. It started using its flippers to wiggle down into the sand.

"I'll go get my sandcastle shovel and help it dig!" said Benny.

"No!" the man shouted. "You might scare it. Turtles always dig nests like this. It knows what it's doing and doesn't need any help."

Other beachgoers started to notice the turtle. Soon at least a dozen people were gathered. The man with the straw hat kept telling the crowd to leave the turtle alone. As more people stopped to look, the man's face started to get red with frustration.

Then a shaggy brown dog wearing a red scarf around its neck ran up. It was panting and dragging a leash. The man grabbed the end of the leash and pulled the dog away just before it got to the turtle.

"Sandy, no!" a woman called as she ran toward the crowd. She was struggling to hold on to several beach bags as she ran. The woman was wearing a bandanna made of the same fabric as the one around the dog's neck.

"Martina, keep better hold of your dog!" the man snapped at her. "I've seen him running loose more than once now. If you can't keep him on a leash, I'll see that he gets banned from the beach."

The woman named Martina took the end of the leash from the man. "He won't hurt the turtles or the eggs," she said. "He's just curious. I know you don't like dogs, Mr. Chatman, but don't assume Sandy is a bad dog because of that."

The man in the straw hat glared at her. "Even if he doesn't *mean* to hurt the turtle, he might scare it. That could make it go back to the water without laying its eggs. Keep him away!"

Not a Bird's Nest

"Come on, Sandy," said Martina. The woman led the dog down the beach and then stopped at a distance to watch the turtle.

As more people joined the crowd, Mr. Chatman's face turned even redder. Violet heard him mumble, "It's no use. There are too many people here now." He took out his cell phone and made a call. "We've got one. Right past mile marker six."

As Mr. Chatman was on the phone, Henry noticed a silver truck coming fast down the beach. Too fast. As it got closer, the driver slowed a little, but only to honk at people to get out of the way. Then it sped away. As the truck passed, Henry noticed a picture on its side door of a fish leaping out of the water. Underneath were the words *Fischer's Custom Fishing Trips.*

"Slow down, Fischer!" Mr. Chatman yelled, shaking his fist at the truck. "Did you see that?" he said to the crowd. "He almost ran over the nest!"

"Does he know there are giant sea turtles here?" Jessie asked.

Mr. Chatman's face was turning very red. "Of course he does! And he knows it's nesting season.

Everyone is supposed to slow down, but he never follows the speed limits."

Violet wanted to know more about the turtle, and even though the man did not seem very friendly, he did seem to know about the animals. "Do you know what kind of turtle this is, Mr. Chatman?" she asked.

"Of course I do," the man said. "Didn't you hear me say I'm a turtle expert?" He waved his hand toward the turtle. "This is called a Kemp's ridley sea turtle, and it's no giant. It's actually the smallest type of sea turtle. But it is much bigger than most land turtles."

Other people in the crowd began to ask questions, which seemed to annoy Mr. Chatman, but he gave good answers.

"I guess he really is a turtle expert," Jessie whispered to her brothers and sister.

"A cranky one!" said Benny.

"Here comes another vehicle," said Henry.

"It's funny looking," said Violet. "It doesn't look big enough to be a real car."

"That is a utility vehicle, a UTV," Mr. Chatman

said. "They are good for getting around the island."

"Wow!" said Benny. "Is that a real park ranger inside?"

The woman driving was wearing a khaki outfit and a ranger-style hat. Her shiny black hair was pulled into a bun. "She's got a badge on," said Henry. "She looks very official."

"That's Ms. Thakur, the ranger I called," said Mr. Chatman. He started waving and yelled, "Over here! Over here!"

The woman stopped the UTV and got out, carrying a bag.

Mr. Chatman kept shouting, even though Jessie didn't think he needed to. The woman was coming toward them as fast as she could.

When the ranger reached the scene, Mr. Chatman started telling her about the truck that had driven down the beach. "You should really have a talk with that Tommy Fischer," he said.

"I thought this was about a turtle, Mr. Chatman," the ranger said.

Mr. Chatman rolled his eyes. "It is, Ms. Thakur. I'm just filling you in on some important information.

The turtle is right over there."

The ranger pulled a pair of rubber gloves out of the bag, put them on, and grabbed a short rope. She walked up to the turtle very slowly, knelt down, and placed the rope at the edge of the hole. The turtle didn't seem to notice. Then Ms. Thakur moved away slowly.

"Why did you put the rope there?" Violet asked.

"It marks the nest," said Ms. Thakur. "If I have to leave before she's finished laying her eggs, I'll know where the nest is when I come back."

Ms. Thakur walked over to Mr. Chatman. "Thank you for calling," she said. "Have you thought about doing our Turtle Patrol training program?"

"I don't have time for any training," Mr. Chatman said. "And I already know all about turtles. It would be a waste of my time."

The ranger raised an eyebrow. "You might be surprised at what you could learn," she said.

The man grumbled and went back to his van. Ms. Thakur turned to the Aldens. "I know Mr. Chatman. But I don't believe I've met you children yet. Where are you from?"

Not a Bird's Nest

Henry told the ranger they were visiting from Connecticut. "We just got here. I can't believe we were lucky enough to see a turtle right away!"

"You've come at a good time of year," Ms. Thakur said. "The females come ashore from April to June to nest. And here's the most amazing part: they come back to the same beaches they were born on!"

Violet looked at the turtle nestled down in the sand. She imagined it returning to this place years after it was born. The turtle had looked so lost coming out of the water. But now Violet saw that the animal knew exactly what it was doing.

"I think she's done laying her eggs," said Ms. Thakur. "Now watch what she does next."

As the children watched, the turtle used her flippers to push sand on top of the eggs. Then she turned around and pulled herself slowly back toward the water. A wave caught the turtle, and within seconds, she had disappeared into the blue water.

"See? She did such a good job covering up the nest, you can't even tell she was here, except for the flipper marks and the rope sticking out." Ms. Thakur went to her vehicle and grabbed a white container and brought it over to the nest. Then she did something Benny did not expect. She started digging up the nest!

When the ranger had dug enough sand so that the eggs were visible, she carefully picked up each one and put it into the cooler. The children could see there was sand in the bottom of the cooler, which helped keep the eggs in place.

"I thought they'd look like bird eggs," Benny said. "These are round like ping-pong balls."

The ranger laughed. "You're right. They do look like ping-pong balls."

"Why are you taking them away?" Violet asked. "Won't the turtle come back to look for them?"

"The mother doesn't come back to the eggs," the ranger explained. "Turtle eggs aren't like bird eggs, where the parents keep them warm. The sand and the sun do that. The eggs hatch on their own, and the little turtles make their way to the ocean all by themselves."

The ranger sighed. "Well, that's the way it's supposed to happen. But these turtles are so endangered that it's important for every egg to hatch. Very few Kemp's ridley sea turtles live long enough to lay their own eggs." She picked up the last egg, placed it in the cooler, and put the lid on.

"Coyotes, raccoons, and even crabs like to eat the eggs. And because vehicles are allowed to drive on the beach, sometimes the sand gets pushed down, and the hatchlings have trouble making it to the ocean. We bring the eggs to our facility so they can be protected until they hatch. Then we release them."

The ranger took out a marker and wrote on a label on the top of the cooler. "We keep track of the date and place we find each nest," she said as she stood up. "Today has been a busy day. I've collected eggs from two other nests, and I had a call about one more."

She put the cooler back in her vehicle. "It's not too far down the beach. Do you children want to watch me collect those eggs too?"

The Aldens all agreed. They were curious to learn more about the turtles. The UTV went slowly, so the children didn't have any trouble keeping up on foot.

A couple hundred feet up the beach, the ranger stopped and got out. She looked around with a frown. "The nest is supposed to be right here," she said. "But I don't see the marker. There should be an orange flag."

"I see something orange over there," Violet said, motioning toward the sand dunes. "It looks like a flag, but it isn't stuck into the ground."

"That's not good," the ranger said, hurrying toward the dunes.

The flag lay near a big hole in the sand, but there were no eggs inside.

"Not again!" the ranger said. "They're gone!"

A Clue in the Night

"What happened to the eggs?" Violet asked.

The children gathered around the empty hole in the sand.

"If an animal dug up the eggs, wouldn't there be broken shells?" Henry asked.

"That's a good observation, Henry," Ms. Thakur said. "Yes, I'm afraid a person dug this nest up."

"Why would someone do that?" asked Jessie.

The ranger sighed. "To sell them, I'm afraid. Because these turtles are endangered, some people will pay a lot of money for the eggs. It's illegal to take them, but poachers do it anyway."

Benny was confused. "What's a poacher?"

"It's someone who takes something that doesn't

belong to them," said Ms. Thakur. "We don't usually have a poaching problem here, but there have been a number of nests that have gone missing recently. Now I know someone is stealing them."

Ms. Thakur looked up and down the beach. "I don't understand how the eggs disappeared so quickly. I got the call an hour ago that the nest had been marked. You didn't see anyone doing anything suspicious, did you?"

"No, we just saw people enjoying the beach," Henry told her.

"What about the man in the truck who was driving too fast?" Violet asked. "He went this way."

"Tommy Fischer?" Ms. Thakur said. "No...no, it couldn't have been him."

Violet thought she sounded very sure about this.

Suddenly the ranger seemed to remember something. "I'm sorry, children, I need to get back to the station."

"Don't you want to try to figure out who did this?" asked Henry.

"Yes...yes, of course," said Ms. Thakur. "But I'm

afraid I have other business to attend to."

"Is there anything we can do to help?" asked Jessie.

"Well, if you'd like, you can stop by the station tomorrow," Ms. Thakur said, getting back into her UTV. "If you don't mind doing a little work on your vacation, you can become official helpers through our junior ranger program."

"Yes!" Violet said. "I want to do that!"

"We'll be there first thing in the morning," Jessie added.

"Good, good," Ms. Thakur said. "See you tomorrow."

With that, Ms. Thakur drove off toward the ranger station. As the children watched the UTV go, Violet said, "I wish Ms. Thakur didn't have to leave. I want to figure out who is taking these eggs."

"She did seem like she was in a hurry to leave after we found the nest," said Henry. "I wonder if she knows more than she told us."

"I'm sure she has a lot to do," said Jessie. "Remember how big and long this island is? That is a lot of land to help take care of."

"You're right, Jessie," said Henry. "Maybe we can help by figuring out what's happening to the eggs on our own."

"A mystery!" said Benny. He looked all around. "But we need clues to solve a mystery. I don't see any clues here."

"We need suspects too," said Violet. "I don't know why the ranger is so sure Mr. Fischer didn't take the eggs. He didn't seem to care much about the turtles the way he was driving."

"That *was* strange," said Jessie. "We should keep an eye on him."

Henry pointed at a group of people sunbathing down the beach. "I have an idea. Whoever is taking the eggs will have to have something to put them in, like that cooler that Ms. Thakur had. We can look for people carrying big containers who don't look like they are out to spend the day on the beach."

"That would be a good clue," Jessie said. "Good thinking, Henry." She noticed the sun was getting lower in the sky. "I didn't realize we'd been gone so long. We should get back."

A Clue in the Night

***

Back at the campsite, Grandfather was waiting. "Time for dinner," he called as they walked up.

Benny rubbed his stomach. "My tummy has been telling me that for hours."

"I was wondering when you'd get back," Grandfather said. "I didn't want to have a feast all by myself. The cooler is full."

Jessie opened the lid. "There's enough food in there for dinner tonight and breakfast and lunch tomorrow," Grandfather said.

Watch wagged his tail. "There's enough for dogs too," Grandfather added.

While Grandfather grilled hot dogs, Violet fed Watch. Henry and Jessie set out the rest of the food, and Benny told Grandfather all about their day.

"I'm glad you got to see a turtle," Grandfather said. "Though it's troubling about the missing eggs. I suspect an animal is digging them up. A clutch of eggs would be a feast for a raccoon."

"I wish it was an animal," Violet said. "Animals don't know that these turtles are endangered. A person stealing the eggs would have to know."

"We think it has to be a person," Jessie said. "The eggs were dug up so quickly, and there weren't any broken shells around."

"We plan to keep a lookout tomorrow," Henry said.

"Well, if anyone can solve the mystery, it will be you four." Grandfather picked up a hot dog with the tongs. "Who wants the first hot dog? Let me guess, Benny?"

"Yes!" Benny said.

After dishing up, the Aldens sat down on a blanket in the sand.

"It's nice eating dinner and watching the waves," Violet said.

"Especially when you have a feast!" said Benny.

By the time the Aldens were finished eating and had cleaned up, the sun had set. Violet looked up at the night sky. "We must be able to see millions and millions of stars," she said. "That's one of the best parts about camping."

Grandfather got up. "Yes, it is, but I think I've seen enough stars for tonight. I'm ready for my nice comfortable bed. Tomorrow I'll pick you up and take you out to dinner at a restaurant.

"Have fun enjoying the beach tomorrow. I have my cell phone if you need anything." He smiled. "I do have a little surprise. I've hired a man to teach you windsurfing. He'll meet you at the campsite at two o'clock. The conditions here are supposed to be excellent for windsurfing."

"That will be terrific!" Henry said.

"Yes, I've always wanted to learn," said Jessie.

After Grandfather left, the children stayed outside a while longer. Benny had a hard time keeping his eyes open. He leaned his head against

Jessie. "The sound of the waves is making me sleepy," he said.

"Me too," Jessie agreed. "I think we should all go to sleep."

The children got ready for bed and climbed into their sleeping bags. Benny was asleep as soon as he closed his eyes.

Sometime later, Benny woke up. At first he thought he was having a dream, but after a moment, he remembered where they were. Benny looked around. Everyone else was sleeping except Watch. He had his head up like he was listening for something. Benny didn't hear anything strange, so he closed his eyes. Then Watch gave a small whine, and Benny opened his eyes again.

"What is it, boy?" Benny whispered. "Remember, there is nothing here to be scared about." Benny wasn't so sure he believed that, but it felt better to say it.

Outside, a dog barked. The sound made Benny jump.

He got up and looked out of the door of the tent. The moon was bright. Benny could see a long way up and down the shoreline. At first he thought the beach was empty. Then he noticed two shapes moving along the water.

As the pair got closer, Benny could see it was a person walking a dog. Benny thought it was a funny time for them to be out on the beach. The dog stopped to dig. Benny heard a woman's voice say, "Good dog."

Watch poked his head out the tent and barked. The other dog started toward the tent like it wanted to come see Watch, but the person pulled the dog's leash to make it walk with her down the beach.

Benny tried to stay up until they moved out of sight, but the sound of the waves made him sleepy again. He zipped up the door of the tent and went back to his sleeping bag. Watch lay down next to him.

Since Watch no longer seemed worried, Benny decided he wasn't either. He closed his eyes.

CHAPTER 4

Real Writing, Real Clue

The next time Benny opened his eyes, it was morning. Once again, no one else was awake except Watch.

"Come on, Watch," Benny whispered. "Let's build a sandcastle while we wait for everyone to get up."

Benny quietly unzipped the tent door and went down to the water. As he worked on his castle, he kept checking the ocean to see if any turtles were coming out of the water. But this time none did.

When the castle was almost finished, Jessie came out of the tent, yawning.

Benny jumped up. "Let's go see Ms. Thakur!" he called. "I want to learn how to be a junior ranger!"

"It's a little early," Jessie said, yawning again. "She's probably not at work yet, and we need to eat breakfast. You'll get hungry if we don't."

The others got up too. Jessie set out some muffins, and they ate their breakfast and watched the birds on the beach.

"I wish I knew the names of all these different kinds," Violet said. "I forgot to bring my bird book."

All of a sudden, the birds scattered. The shaggy dog the Aldens had seen the day before came running down the beach, dragging his leash while he chased the birds. Today, Sandy had a purple bandanna around his neck instead of a red one. Martina, the dog's owner, again came running after him. She was wearing a matching purple bandanna and carrying several beach bags.

Martina caught up to Sandy as he was digging a hole in the sand. She grabbed his leash, but after only a few seconds seemed to forget about it. She dropped the leash as she searched through one of her bags. After a little while, Sandy took off running, chasing more birds. Jessie was about to call to Martina to tell her the dog was getting away when Martina noticed and ran after him.

Seeing the two of them reminded Benny of the night before. Sandy was about the same size as the dog he had seen on the beach. But Sandy didn't seem to be as well trained as that dog. Benny told the others what he had seen.

When he was done, Violet asked, "Why would Martina walk her dog in the middle of the night? Do you think it might have something to do with the turtle eggs going missing?"

"I don't know," said Henry. "From the way Mr. Chatman talked, Martina seems to be on the beach a lot."

"That's true," said Jessie. "But there are lots of reasons why she might be on the beach. It isn't against the rules to be out at night."

Jessie's words made Violet feel better. She hoped Sandy and Martina weren't the ones taking the turtle eggs. But she knew she could not be sure. "I just wish Martina would keep hold of Sandy's leash," she said. "Who knows what he might get into when he's running free."

The children walked to the ranger station. On the

way, they passed Mr. Chatman. He was talking to a couple who were carrying beach chairs, lecturing them about the tides. Mr. Chatman glanced at the Aldens but acted like he didn't recognize them.

Violet didn't mind. She did not like how the man had yelled at them the day before.

The ranger station was attached to the visitor center. Violet tied Watch's leash to a railing on the deck, and they walked in the main entrance. Inside was a gift shop, which had posters on the walls of all the different kinds of birds and shells on Padre Island.

"It's amazing such a small place has so many different birds and animals," Violet said as she studied one of the posters. "I wish I could see them all."

An older man stood behind a counter, arranging postcards. "Good morning," he called out to them.

Jessie walked up to the counter. She saw that the man's name tag said *Leo Halprin, Volunteer*. "Hello," she said. "We met Ms. Thakur yesterday on the beach. She said to stop by this morning so we could go through the junior ranger program."

The man smiled. "Excellent! We always need more rangers. I'll check to see where she is and when she'll be back." The man spoke into a walkie-talkie. Then he listened and set it back down. "You're in luck. She'll be back in a few minutes. You can wait in her office if you'd like."

Ms. Thakur's office was small and crowded with books. Most of them were nature guides about the birds, plants, and animals.

Henry noticed a colorful brochure on the ranger's desk. It had a picture of a leaping fish on it. "That's the same picture of the fish we saw yesterday," he said. "It was on the truck that was going too fast." Henry leaned closer. "It's a brochure for Mr. Fischer's business."

There was a yellow sticky note on the brochure. The words on the note were written in big, swooping letters.

"Is that real writing?" Benny asked. "I can't read any of it."

"It's real writing," Jessie said. "It's just extra fancy. It says, *We should talk. I know how you can make more money.*"

"Why would Mr. Fischer want to help Ms. Thakur make more money?" Henry asked. "And why would he give her a brochure? If she wanted to go fishing, she probably already knows the places to go."

"I don't understand how a fishing guide can help a park ranger make money," Violet said. "I wonder if this has something to do with why Ms. Thakur left so suddenly yesterday."

Just as Violet finished speaking, the door opened. "Good morning!" said Ms. Thakur.

CHAPTER 5

Rangers on Patrol

Violet jumped at the sound of the ranger's voice. She hoped Ms. Thakur hadn't noticed them looking at the brochure. Violet didn't want the ranger to think they'd been snooping around her office.

Ms. Thakur went around and sat behind her desk. She opened a drawer and took out four booklets. "I'm so glad you came in," she said cheerfully. "We need all the help we can get! These are the booklets I was telling you about. You can sit out on the porch and work on them, and if you finish them before I leave, I can swear you in. You can be official junior rangers this very morning."

"Yes!" said Benny. "I want to be a junior ranger right away!"

"We all do," said Jessie.

"Wonderful. Let's get you some pencils." They followed the ranger out of her office. "Leo, would you lend these future rangers some pencils?"

The man handed them four pencils.

"Just bring them back in when you are finished," Ms. Thakur said.

The children went to the porch and sat down at a picnic bench. The booklets were very interesting. Jessie helped Benny read some of the words.

"I like that there are pictures of different kind of shells with their names listed," said Violet. "I'm going to try to find one of each kind for my collection."

"I'd like to see some of the animals that live here," said Henry. "It says many of them are nocturnal though. It's probably hard to spot them in the dark. I'm sure if raccoons or coyotes were digging up the eggs, that would be the time when they would do it."

The children worked through each page. When they were finished, they took the booklets inside and gave Leo the pencils. The ranger came out of her office. "Perfect timing," she said. "How did you do?"

"We're all done!" Benny blurted.

"Excellent! Come over here and line up. Now raise your hands and repeat after me: 'I am proud to be a National Park Service Junior Ranger. I promise to appreciate, respect, and protect all national parks. I also promise to continue learning about the landscape, plants, animals, and history of these special places. I will share what I learn with my friends and family.'"

The Aldens repeated the words. The ranger smiled. "I declare you junior rangers."

Leo took four park ranger hats from behind the counter and handed them to the children. Then he handed out four badges, each with a picture of a sea turtle and the words *Junior Ranger, Padre Island*.

Benny was so excited, he had trouble putting his pin onto his shirt, so Jessie helped him. "I'm going to wear it every day!" Benny said. "Even when we get back home."

"I hope you do," said Ms. Thakur. "Now I need to go out on turtle patrol. My new junior rangers can come along if they'd like."

Violet got Watch, and they all followed Ms.

Thakur to the beach. It was a nice day but very windy. Benny's hat blew off, and he had to chase it down. They had gone only a short way before Henry noticed something.

"Are those turtle tracks?" he asked, motioning to two sets of marks in the sand.

"Good eyes," the ranger said. "They definitely are."

Jessie followed the tracks up toward the dunes. "I don't see a turtle," she called.

"It's already come and gone," Ms. Thakur said as she followed Jessie. "I hope the eggs are still there." The ranger knelt down and dug very slowly. Violet thought it felt like they stood there for a long time.

Finally, Ms. Thakur announced, "They're here. Would one of you get a cooler from the UTV?"

Jessie ran to get it, and the ranger started collecting the eggs just as she had done the day before. Before Ms. Thakur was finished, Martina and Sandy approached, and Sandy started to dig a few feet away from the nest.

This time, Martina was holding Sandy's leash, and she pulled him back.

"Look!" said Benny. "Sandy found something!"

"It's a little red plastic ball," Violet said.

Sandy barked and wagged his tail. "Good dog," Martina said. She rubbed the dog's head and then put the ball into one of her many bags.

Again, Benny thought back to the night before.

This time there was no mistaking the voice. It *had* been Martina and Sandy walking along the shoreline!

"Sandy sure likes to dig," Benny said. "He must be good at finding things."

"Yes, he..." Martina trailed off. "I mean, maybe he is...I can't say I've ever noticed."

Benny wanted to ask Martina more about how Sandy had found the red ball. And about why they had been out in the middle of the night. But before he could, Ms. Thakur spoke, "See what I'm doing?" The ranger was moving the last couple of eggs from the nest to the cooler. "This is very important. I'm not turning the eggs over. We need to keep them right side up. If they aren't kept this way, they might not hatch."

Ms. Thakur finished explaining the process, and then Martina and Sandy continued down the beach. The children followed the ranger back to the UTV. As they went, Benny noticed the turtle tracks had disappeared. "Where'd they go?" he asked, looking around.

"The wind blows the sand and erases the tracks,"

Ms. Thakur explained. "It makes it very hard to find nests that aren't marked. That's why we put the rope into the nesting site or mark them with flags." She lifted the cooler into the back of her vehicle. "Would you like to see the incubation area? It's my favorite place in the station. You can learn a lot more about the turtles."

"Yes!" Jessie said. "We'd like that."

"Terrific! Meet me back there, and I'll show you around." The ranger drove off, and the Aldens walked back in the direction of the station.

When the children got there, they tied Watch's leash to the railing. He lay down to wait for them. Inside, Leo led them into a back room where Ms. Thakur was working. It was full of different kinds of equipment and containers.

"It takes quite an effort to get them to hatch," Ms. Thakur said. "When we have eggs here, we sometimes take turns spending the night. We get up every few hours and spritz water on them. The ones nearing the end of the incubation period need fans put on them. We also monitor temperatures and check to see if any eggs are close to hatching."

"That is a lot of work, but it sounds exciting," Jessie said.

"It is very exciting," said Ms. Thakur. "And it's interesting to watch. Each baby turtle has one small tooth, called a caruncle, just to help them break out of the shell. Since we hatch the eggs here, the turtles get a little time to rest after all that effort. Then we release them at the beach."

Ms. Thakur checked a thermometer on one of the containers and wrote a number on her clipboard. "I've got some paperwork I have to do. Thank you all for your help. If you want to keep looking for turtles, there are some orange flags in a bucket on the front porch. You can take a few." She pulled a card out of her pocket. "If you spot a turtle, mark the nest, and then call this number. A ranger will come out and take care of the eggs."

The children walked toward the main entrance. "Can we look at the guidebooks before we go to the beach?" Violet asked. "I want to see if they have one about the birds on Padre Island."

While they were looking at the display of books, the front door opened. Martina and Sandy came in.

Martina didn't notice them. She walked up to the counter and spoke to Leo. Because the store was so small, the children couldn't help but overhear her.

"I'd like to buy one of those white foam containers the rangers use," Martina said.

"I'm sorry. We don't sell those," Leo told her. "We have our own supply for the eggs, but we get them in town. I'm sure you could find one at a store there."

"I really want one just like yours," Martina said. "A used one would be perfect. I'll pay extra for it."

Leo shook his head. "I'm sorry. We don't have any for sale, new or used."

"That's too bad," Martina said. She sounded disappointed. "I could really use one."

"I'm sorry," the man said again.

Martina frowned. "Come on, Sandy," she said, and then she turned and left without another word.

Once Violet had paid for her book, the Aldens went outside too.

"I wonder why Martina wanted a cooler so badly," Jessie said, untying Watch from the porch.

"Maybe she wanted a container to keep all the

things she found on the beach in," Violet suggested.

Henry got two orange flags out of the bucket. "Maybe. It *is* strange though. If she is the person taking the eggs, it would be much easier to carry them in a cooler than in one of her bags."

"That's not the only thing," said Benny. "When Martina was talking, I recognized her voice from last night. I think it *was* her and Sandy on the beach!"

"Something strange is going on," said Jessie. "But we still need more information before we can come to any conclusions."

Henry nodded. "In the meantime, let's go save some turtles!"

CHAPTER

6

Too Many Suspects

The beach was crowded. There were people hunting for shells. Others were sunbathing or building sandcastles. A few people were fishing.

"There are so many people out today, it's going to be hard to figure out who we should suspect," said Jessie.

"I'll be able to tell," Benny said. "Anyone who steals turtle eggs must be mean, and they'll have a mean face too."

"I don't know about that, Benny," Henry said. "But we will keep looking."

Jessie stopped to take a picture of the beach. As she did, a motion in the viewfinder caught her attention. She zoomed the lens in on it. "I see a turtle up ahead!" Jessie said. "It's heading into the water."

The Aldens hurried toward the spot where the turtle gone into the ocean. Then they followed the tracks up toward the sand dunes. The tracks stopped at a smooth area that looked exactly like what they'd seen at the other turtle nest.

Jessie took out her cell phone. "I'll call Ms. Thakur."

Watch edged in to sniff around at the nest, but Violet held him back.

"I suppose all dogs can smell that a turtle has been here," Henry said. "And coyotes too. It's probably easy for either of them to find the eggs."

"I hear a car coming," Violet said. She looked up the beach and saw the silver truck from the day before. Again, it was racing toward them.

Jessie took hold of Benny's hand. "We should move back," she said. "He's driving so fast, it's like he doesn't even see us." The Aldens moved closer to the turtle nest. The truck did slow down as it passed them. There was a man driving and two women in the truck. The man leaned out the window. "Don't stand in the tracks for vehicles," he shouted. "You're slowing people down!"

The truck sped away just as Ms. Thakur arrived.

"That Mr. Fischer acts like he owns the beach!" Violet cried.

"Don't pay any attention to Tommy," Ms. Thakur said. "He is only thinking about getting his customers to the best fishing spots. Now, I need to get these eggs out of the nest and back to the incubation area."

Jessie was surprised that Ms. Thakur wasn't more upset by the way Tommy Fischer broke the rules on the beach. She thought back to the note on the brochure they'd seen on the ranger's desk. What was going on between them?

The ranger collected the eggs and put the cooler into her vehicle. "You four are already proving to be excellent junior rangers!" she called as she drove off. As with the day before, it seemed like she was in a hurry to get somewhere.

"We should go eat lunch," Jessie said. "We need to be ready when the windsurfer instructor meets us."

The Aldens headed back to their campsite. They ate quickly and finished their meal just as the instructor pulled up.

The young man introduced himself as Finn. "Your grandfather told me all your names." He turned to Benny. "I'm sorry, Benny. Your grandfather didn't know you have to be eight years old to take a lesson, but he suggested we split up the lessons so someone can stay with you while I take the others out. Then we'll switch."

"I'll stay with Benny first," Henry said. "We can build a giant sandcastle together."

"Sounds good," the instructor said. "Girls, let's drive a little farther down the beach. There's a spot where the water is the perfect depth for your first lesson."

After Jessie and Violet had gone, Henry and Benny found a place to build their sandcastle.

They worked for a long time, with Watch laying in the sand beside them. After a while, a silver truck pulled up. It was Tommy Fischer. But instead of the two woman they had seen him with earlier, he was now with a father and son. The boy looked only a little older than Benny.

"This should be a better fishing spot," Tommy

said to the pair. He took fishing rods and other supplies out of the back of his vehicle and showed the pair what to do.

The father and son cast their lines into the surf. Benny and Henry kept working on their sandcastle. Henry looked up from time to time to watch the fishermen. He didn't see anyone catch anything.

After a while, the boy said, "This is boring. I thought we were going to catch buckets of fish."

"We almost always catch something here," Tommy told him. "I guess it's just a bad day today."

After a few more tries, the boy set down his rod. He came over to Benny and Henry. "Can I help you?" he asked.

"Sure," Benny said. "You can make a big tower right here if you want."

The boy worked on the tower for a while, but then he got up again and went down to the water.

"Look at all the birds!" he called, pointing to the small brown and white birds poking their beaks down into the wet sand. "What kind are they?" he asked Tommy.

"Uh...I...I don't know," Tommy said.

"They're funny!" the boy said, running toward them and flapping his arms. The birds scurried away from him. The boy walked back to Tommy.

"I heard there were turtles here," he said. "Can you show us some turtles?"

Tommy shook his head. "I'm sorry. I just do fishing."

The boy came back and worked on the tower for a little while. Then he said, "Dad, I'm hungry."

"We already ate all the snacks we brought. You don't have any, do you?" the father asked Tommy.

Tommy shook his head. "No, I'm sorry. Fishing guides aren't allowed to sell food in the park. It's against the rules."

A few minutes later, the father handed Tommy his fishing rod. "We're done fishing," he said. "We'll go find some food and then find something else to do. It's not worth our time standing out here all day if we don't catch any fish. We'd like our money back."

Tommy tried to talk them into trying another fishing spot, but the man refused. "I'm sorry. I can't give refunds," Tommy said. "I can't guarantee people will catch fish."

The man looked upset. "Just take us back to our car then," he said.

The boy and his father got into Tommy's truck, so Henry and Benny couldn't hear any more of the conversation.

"It's too bad," Henry said. "It wasn't Tommy's fault they didn't catch any fish. I've been fishing a lot of times when I didn't catch anything."

"I still don't like him," Benny said. "He has a mean face."

Henry gave Benny a disapproving look.

"Plus, he drives all over with that big truck," Benny continued. "It would be easy for him to hide the turtle eggs in the back."

"That part is true," said Henry. "And there was that strange note in Ms. Thakur's office. If Tommy's business isn't doing well, he might be selling the eggs to make more money. Maybe Ms. Thakur is helping him."

Benny looked down at his junior ranger badge. "I didn't think of that," said Benny. "That would make me sad."

Henry patted him on the shoulder. "We don't

know anything yet for sure."

Just then the windsurfing instructor drove up with Jessie and Violet. "It was awesome!" Jessie said.

"Windsurfing is hard but fun," Violet added. "You'll like it, Henry."

While Henry went with Finn, Jessie helped Benny with his sandcastle. Violet collected shells. Watch dug around next to the castle for a little while, then lay back down. Whenever someone walked by, Jessie looked to see if the person was carrying a cooler. Several people were, but no one seemed to be acting strangely.

It wasn't long before Martina and Sandy came walking down the beach. Martina stopped a short distance away and bent down to pick up a shell. She seemed excited by what she found and began collecting others. Setting down her bags, she told Sandy to sit, and he did.

After having seen Sandy run away from Martina so many times, Violet was surprised to see the dog obey his owner. When Martina had collected quite a few shells, she sat down and pulled a small, flat piece of wood out of one of the bags. Violet watched as Martina sorted through the shells, setting some aside and laying others on the board.

Violet was very curious about what the woman was doing. She walked over. "Are you making something?" she asked.

Martina looked up and smiled. "Watch this." She added a few more shells to the board.

"You made a sea turtle out of shells!" said Violet.

"Yes, I love to make sea turtle pictures with shells. I make bird pictures too. There are more than three hundred different species here, and I'm planning to make pictures of all of them."

"I like birds too!" Violet said. "What are you going to do with this picture? The shells aren't stuck down."

"I lay them out to make sure I have all the shells I need," Martina explained. "Then I'll put those in a separate bag. When I get back to my apartment, I'll lay them out again and fasten them down."

"Couldn't you glue them on here?" Violet asked.

"I could, but sand gets in the glue," Martina said. "The pictures don't look as good when they dry, and the sand makes the glue cloudy."

Two women walked by and noticed what Martina was doing. They came over to watch.

"Do you sell those?" one of the women asked. "I'd love to get a good souvenir to take home to my sister."

"I do sell them," Martina said. "I mean, I would sell them if I could." She sounded flustered. "I don't have a shop or anything, but I have several that are ready to hang on the wall."

"Can we see them?" the woman asked.

"I'm so sorry," Martina said, "but they are back at my apartment."

The woman looked disappointed. "Oh, that's too bad. One of these would be perfect for my sister."

All of a sudden, Martina smiled. "I have an idea. If you are going to be on the beach for a few more hours, I can go get some and meet you when you are ready to leave. There's a restaurant by the causeway called the Laughing Gull. We could meet in the parking lot there, and you could see if you like any of them."

"That would be terrific!" the woman said. "We're

going to leave here about six thirty. Can you meet us then?"

"I'll be there," said Martina.

"Wonderful!" said the woman. "We'll see you then."

Martina's smile grew bigger as the women walked away. She leaned over and ruffled Sandy's ears. "I'll buy you a treat with the money!" she said to the dog.

"It's exciting you are going to sell some of your artwork," Violet said. "I bet you could sell lots of these to tourists."

"I could if I had a place to display them, like a shop. But it costs too much money to rent one." Martina sighed. "Maybe someday." She loaded her supplies back in her bag. "I should go so I can get the pictures and meet those people on time. Come along, Sandy. Nice talking to you," she said to Violet.

Soon after Martina and Sandy left, Henry and the instructor returned.

"We're running a little late, so it's time to go," Finn called out the car window. "I promised your grandfather I'd get you back to the campsite in time for you to change to go to dinner."

Jessie, Violet, and Benny packed up their beach supplies and climbed in. After the instructor dropped them off, it didn't take long for them to get ready.

"Watch will have to stay in the tent," Henry said, "but he should be tired out from being on the beach all day." Watch didn't seem to mind. As soon as Henry put him inside, he lay down and closed his eyes.

While the children waited for Grandfather, Jessie asked Henry and Benny if they had seen anything strange while she and Violet had been windsurfing.

But before Henry could say anything, Benny said, "Can we wait until after dinner to talk about clues? All I can think about is cheeseburgers."

Jessie laughed. "Okay, Benny, we can wait until after dinner to talk about clues. There's Grandfather now!"

CHAPTER 7

The Expert at the Restaurant

"I hope this restaurant is a good one," Grandfather said when they got into the car. "The owner of the inn recommended it to me. It's supposed to have wonderful food and a great view of the ocean."

As they drove, the children told Grandfather all about the turtles. They had so much to tell they were still talking when Grandfather got to the causeway.

"Is that the restaurant?" Jessie asked, noticing a big white building close to the water. "The Laughing Gull? A woman we met on the beach mentioned it."

"That's it," Grandfather said. "It has quite a view. The side that faces the water is almost all windows."

Grandfather parked at the back of the building,

and together the Aldens walked around to the entrance. "Look," said Henry, pointing to a small building across the street. "That must be Tommy Fischer's office." The small wooden building had a big sign across the top with the picture of the leaping fish. Henry explained to Grandfather about Mr. Fischer and his driving.

"He doesn't seem very nice," Benny said. "He yelled at us."

There was a light on inside the building, and they could see Mr. Fischer sitting behind a counter. He had his head propped up with one hand and his eyes closed. "It looks like he's asleep," Violet said.

"That's funny," Benny said. "He should go home."

"It looks like he's in the middle of doing some work, judging by that big stack of paper in front of him," Grandfather said. "I suppose he's tired at the end of the day. It's hard work running a business."

When the Aldens reached the entrance of the restaurant, a big group had just gone in but had stopped on the other side of the doorway. One of the men said, "This restaurant is too fancy. Let's eat someplace more casual." He pointed down to his flip-flops. "I don't think they'd want us in here."

The hostess said, "Please, stay. We don't have a dress code. You're fine."

"No," the man said. "This wasn't the kind of restaurant we were looking for." The group walked out.

"Is it too fancy for us too?"' Benny asked Grandfather.

"No, we're fine," Grandfather said.

The hostess gave the Aldens a big smile when they came in. "You can pick where you'd like to sit. As you can see, we're not busy."

The Aldens picked a table. "It *is* a fancy restaurant with the white tablecloths and chandeliers," Violet said. She didn't say it out loud, but she didn't like the way the restaurant had been decorated. The walls and the chairs were gray, and it made the whole place seem gloomy.

The back section of the restaurant was roped off, and there were stacks of supplies sitting on the floor. A glass tank covered a big stretch of the wall.

"It looks like they are putting in a big aquarium," Henry said.

Grandfather picked up his napkin. "An aquarium will be a nice touch. It will brighten up the place a bit."

A woman carrying menus came over to their table. "I'm sorry about the construction," she said. "The new aquarium is almost done. The water is in, and some of the fish will go in tomorrow."

"I've never seen an aquarium that big," Henry said. "It's going to take up almost the whole wall."

"The owner loves tropical fish. He's an expert in them." She lowered her voice. "If he comes in tonight, just don't ask him any questions about the fish unless you want an earful of information. He likes to talk, and once he gets started, you'll never get away."

The Aldens' food arrived quickly. Benny and Violet's meals came in baskets that looked like little boats.

"You can take the baskets with you when you leave if you want to play with them later," the server told them.

"I like this place!" said Benny. He pretended to drive the boat around the table.

Henry took a bite of his meal. "The food *is* really good," he said.

"It's too bad they don't have more customers," Jessie said.

It didn't take long for everyone to eat. "I guess you were all very hungry," the server said as she collected the empty plates.

"We were." Benny picked up his boat. "If we come back, do I get another boat?"

"Of course! A boat at each visit!" the server said. "And if you come back, you'll get to see the fish!"

After Grandfather paid the bill, the Aldens walked out of the restaurant and around to the parking lot. Tommy Fischer's office was dark. "It appears that fellow has finally gone home," Grandfather said. "I bet he'll be right back at work first thing tomorrow morning. People who own small businesses put in a lot of hours."

When they reached the parking lot, the Aldens had to wait to get to their car as a big white van pulled up and parked at the back entrance of the restaurant. The area wasn't very well lit, but they saw a man in a large straw hat get out and hurry in the door. It had a sign on it that said Employees Only.

"Wasn't that Mr. Chatman?" Jessie asked. "He's a man we saw on the beach," she explained to Grandfather. "He knows a lot about sea turtles."

"Yes, that was him," Henry said. "He must work at the restaurant. I wonder why he's coming to work so late."

"I suppose he's getting food ready for tomorrow," Grandfather said as he got in the car. "I like this place. We'll definitely have to come back to see the fish."

After Grandfather dropped them off at the campsite, Jessie looked through their supplies. "I think we need some dessert. How about roasting marshmallows?"

"Yes!" Benny said.

Once the fire was ready, Benny toasted a marshmallow just a little and then ate it quickly.

"Well, Benny, now that you've had dinner *and* dessert, can we talk about clues?"

"Mm-hmm," said Benny, his mouth full of marshmallow.

Jessie told Henry what she and Violet had

learned while he was windsurfing.

Henry poked the fire with a stick. "So Martina makes artwork with the shells she finds on the beach? That explains why she is always on the beach. But we still don't know why she needed one of those coolers from the ranger station so badly."

"Or why she was walking down the beach in the middle of the night," said Benny. "Was she looking for night shells?"

Jessie laughed. "I think the shells at night are the same ones during the day."

"Benny and I learned something today too," said Henry. He told Jessie and Violet about Tommy Fischer and his unhappy customers.

When he was done, Violet said, "Maybe that's why Mr. Fischer is in such a rush all the time. His business is doing poorly. Grandfather did say that owning a business is hard work."

"But if his business isn't doing well, why would he ask Ms. Thakur if she wanted to *make* money?" Jessie wondered, remembering the note they had found in the ranger's office. "Wouldn't he be the one who needed money?"

The Expert at the Restaurant

The children sat looking at the fire, thinking about Jessie's question. Then Benny said, "What about Mr. Chatman? He knows a lot about the turtles. Maybe he took them."

Violet thought back to the first time they met Mr. Chatman. "Did you notice how he didn't seem to want anyone around when we found that nest? Maybe he wanted to take the eggs for himself."

"That was strange," said Henry. "It seems like we have a lot of questions and not many answers, and I don't think we'll find any more clues tonight. Let's get to sleep and keep an eye out for more clues tomorrow."

But the children did not need to wait until the morning to find another clue.

Turtles Everywhere

Henry, Jessie, Violet, and Benny fell asleep as quickly as they had the night before.

And just like the night before, a noise outside made Watch perk his ears up. This time it was Violet who woke up with him. She heard a sound coming from a vehicle outside. It seemed too late for a car to be driving around, but then she remembered the ranger had said people stayed over at the station to watch the turtle eggs.

Watch was facing the door of the tent, listening carefully. Violet decided she wanted to make sure it was turtle helpers, so she got up and looked out. There was a light flickering outside the back of the building. It looked like a flashlight.

Suddenly, a loud clanging noise rang out from the ranger station. It was so loud Violet jumped.

Before she could decide what to do, Violet saw a person come around the corner of the building carrying something in both arms. The person carefully put the object into the back of a small car and got into the driver's seat. The car drove away.

Violet kept watching, but there was no more activity at the station. She went back into her sleeping bag, deciding it wouldn't do any good to wake the others up. The car was already gone.

The next morning, Violet told the others what she had seen.

"We should tell Ms. Thakur," Henry said. "It sounds like someone was trying to break into the station."

"I hope no eggs are missing!" Benny said.

After breakfast they hurried to find the ranger. Violet told her about the nighttime visitor.

Surprisingly, Ms. Thakur didn't seem concerned. "There's no sign of a break-in. Sometimes people just like to walk at night and look at the stars. They may have come up to the building to read the signs about when we're open so they could know when to come back."

"But I heard a clanging noise, and the person left carrying something," Violet said.

Ms. Thakur thought for a moment. "The dumpster is behind the building. The noise could have been the sound of the lid closing. It's very loud. I don't know what anyone would want from the dumpster though. Our garbage is mostly things we can't recycle like broken coolers and some of the used containers from the incubation area. Whatever it was, I wouldn't worry about it."

The walkie-talkie on the ranger's belt buzzed. She pulled it off and listened. When she was finished, she told the children, "It's supposed to be a very windy and wavy day. That means something very exciting might happen. Those are perfect conditions for what's called an *arribada*, a big nesting event. If we're lucky, many turtles may come ashore today, and that means we have lots of eggs to collect. It's all hands on deck!"

"Yay!" said Benny. "I want to see turtles every-where!"

They followed Ms. Thakur down the beach to a spot where dozens of volunteers and a few park rangers had gathered. Ms. Thakur got everyone's attention. "The volunteers will spread out up and down the beach. If you see a turtle come ashore, wait until it's finished laying its eggs, then mark the spot with a flag and call it in. Everyone take a few flags. The park rangers will come around and collect the eggs."

"There's one already!" Benny pointed.

"And there's another," Jessie said. "Look at all of them coming in!"

The other rangers and the volunteers moved closer to the turtles.

Ms. Thakur came over to the children. "You Aldens make a good team. Why don't you come up to marker two and patrol the area between two and three?"

The children headed off, eager to get started.

"At least no eggs will disappear today with all the people around," Violet said.

"Yes, that's a relief," Jessie agreed.

"Hey, isn't that Mr. Chatman?" Henry asked. He pointed at a man in big straw hat sitting in a beach chair next to a big white van. A cooler sat nearby. The man didn't look up from the book he was reading as the children passed by.

The wind picked up. Jessie shivered. "I'm surprised Mr. Chatman is out here. It's not a very good day to sit on the beach."

Turtles Everywhere

"I wonder why he isn't helping," Violet said.

"I don't know. He's missing out on all the fun. Let's go faster," Henry said. "I don't want to miss any turtles."

As soon as they got to their assigned marker, Violet spotted a turtle. Over the next few hours, they patrolled their stretch of the beach and found three more nests, marking each one with a flag.

"The rangers are going to be busy collecting all of these eggs," Jessie said. "We should go back the other way in case more turtles came in after we passed by."

Henry looked up the beach to see if any rangers were close to their area. He saw a person, but it wasn't a ranger. It was Martina and Sandy.

The two were walking very slowly. Both the woman and the dog had their heads down like they were looking for something. Martina was carrying bags again.

"We're finding lots of turtle nests!" Benny called out as they got closer. When Martina and Sandy reached them, Sandy flopped down in the sand. Watch came over and gave a short bark and then danced away like he wanted Sandy to play.

Sandy put his head down on his paws.

"Is Sandy okay?" Henry asked.

Martina sighed. "I'm afraid Sandy got away from me again today. He ran out of sight, and it took me a long time to find him. He's all tired out from his adventures. I'm tired from chasing him."

She urged Sandy to get back up. "We can't stay and chat. I want to get these heavy bags of shells back to my car."

"I hope she just had shells in those bags," Jessie said as she watched the woman walk away.

"There's a ranger coming," Henry said.

It was Ms. Thakur. "Any luck?" she called out.

"Yes! The first flag is right over here!" Violet said, hurrying to show the ranger the right spot. When Violet got there, she realized something was wrong. The flag was missing!

"Over here," Benny called. He was standing next to the flag, which was laying on its side in the sand.

"That's not where we put it!" said Violet. "We put it right here. I remember because it was by the dune with the mix of yellow and white flowers."

Turtles Everywhere

Jessie walked over to where Violet stood. "Someone has been digging here," Jessie said.

"Oh no!" Violet cried.

"And I see animal prints." Henry pointed to a spot near the empty nest. "They look like dog prints, or maybe coyote."

The ranger bent down to look at them. "These are definitely dog prints. See, the toe parts of the print are round. Coyote prints would be more oval." With her finger, she drew a footprint in the sand. "This is what a coyote print looks like. You can tell the ones here are from a dog."

Violet walked in a circle farther out from the nest. "There is a car track here. It's closer to the dunes than the other tracks."

"I'm afraid it's definitely poachers," the ranger said. "We'd better check the other locations you marked."

The flags on the other three nests had all been moved, and all the eggs were missing.

"I can't believe it!" Henry said. "How did someone get those eggs without us noticing?"

But Ms. Thakur didn't seem to be listening. She

was looking down the beach at an approaching truck. It was Tommy Fischer. When he passed, he waved and the ranger waved back. He didn't have any customers with him today.

"I need to check some areas farther down the beach," the ranger said. "I'll see you all later." She hopped in her UTV and drove off after the fishing guide.

Jessie watched her drive away. "That's odd. The ranger stopped paying attention to the missing eggs as soon as Mr. Fischer drove by."

Benny looked down at where the nest had been. "If those are dog prints, does that mean it's Martina and Sandy who are taking the eggs?" he asked.

"I don't know. We've never seen Martina driving a car on the beach," Henry said.

"She has a car that she must park somewhere close to here," Jessie said. She explained about Martina meeting the women to show them her artwork.

"I hope it's not her," Violet said. She felt very discouraged.

The wind blew harder, and it began to rain.

Benny wrapped his arms around himself. He was getting cold.

Jessie's phone rang. It was Grandfather. Jessie put it on speaker so everyone could hear.

"It's not a good day for a cookout," Grandfather said. "Why don't I pick you up and we go to the restaurant we went to last night?"

The children all agreed. It was time to get indoors. They hurried back to the campsite.

After such a chilly afternoon, Grandfather's car felt nice and warm. When they reached the restaurant parking lot, Jessie noticed a woman in a yellow raincoat with the hood up. The woman went up the steps to the back door of the restaurant and knocked.

The rain was falling hard, and Jessie could just barely see someone open the door and hand the woman a small cooler. The woman hurried back to her car. Jessie told the others what she had seen, but the woman was already driving away, and it was too dark to see her face.

"There are coolers everywhere!" Benny said. Henry explained to Grandfather why they were looking out for people with coolers.

"That is a big problem when you are trying to solve a mystery on a beach," Grandfather said. "I think you need a good meal now. Maybe another way to solve the mystery will come to you after you eat."

When the Aldens got inside, they saw the restaurant was even more empty than the night before.

"I guess it's good for us that it's not crowded," Grandfather said. "I don't know how they stay in business though."

"I'm glad you are back!" the hostess said. "We have some amazing specials tonight."

The Aldens picked a table and sat down. Violet looked around. With the rain hitting the windows, the restaurant seemed even gloomier. "At least there are some fish in the aquarium today," she said. About a dozen small fish darted around in the water.

"I wonder how many they're going to add," Henry said. "There's room in that big of a tank for a lot more."

"Isn't that Mr. Chatman?" Violet asked. She

nodded toward a bald man standing by the fish tank, talking to one of the servers.

"I think so, even though he looks different without his hat," Jessie said.

A few more people came into the restaurant. Some went to look at the aquarium, and Mr. Chatman lectured them on the different species. He talked so much that people had to interrupt him to say they wanted to go back to their tables to eat.

"He knows as much about fish as he knows about turtles," Violet whispered to the others.

"Is that man one of the employees here?" Jessie asked the server when she came to take their order.

"That's the owner of the restaurant," the server replied.

"Hi, Mr. Chatman!" Benny called and waved.

Mr. Chatman looked in their direction and frowned.

"He doesn't seem happy to see us," Violet said.

"Mr. Chatman, come meet Grandfather," Benny said.

The man walked over to their table. Henry

introduced him to Grandfather.

"Mr. Chatman is a turtle expert," Benny announced. "He knows everything!" The restaurant owner smiled at that. Violet thought he looked a little friendlier when he smiled.

"Did you help with the arribada?" Jessie asked. "It was amazing."

Mr. Chatman shook his head. "I was far too busy here."

Jessie and Henry looked at each other. "We...we thought we saw you sitting on the beach," Henry said.

Mr. Chatman's smile disappeared. He shifted around and clasped his hands together. "It must have been someone who looked like me. I was here. Running a business takes too much work for me to be lounging on the beach. In fact, I have to get back to the kitchen right now." He hurried away and went through the kitchen doors.

"But it was him on the beach," Benny said. "Why did he lie?"

"I don't know," Jessie said. "That was strange."

The Aldens' food arrived quickly. The meal was

as good as the one they'd eaten the night before, but Benny began to yawn even before he was finished.

"It seems like you've had another very busy day," Grandfather said. "We should go."

Grandfather took them back to their campsite. It had stopped raining and turned into a nice night. "Enjoy tomorrow," he said as they got out of the car. "Remember, we need to leave the day after that."

Grandfather drove off, and Henry opened the flap of the tent to let Watch out. "I wish we didn't have to leave so soon," he said. "I really wanted to figure out who was stealing the eggs."

"We still have tomorrow," Violet said, though she didn't feel very sure they would solve the mystery. There were still a lot of questions to answer.

"I'm not tired anymore. Can we have another fire?" Benny asked. "If we're leaving soon, we'd better use up all the marshmallows."

Jessie laughed. "You're right. They do need to be used up."

The children lit the fire and started roasting marshmallows. It was quiet on the beach. Even though it had stopped raining, the Aldens didn't see as many people as they had the other nights.

"Isn't that Mr. Fischer's truck outside the ranger station?" Henry asked. "What's he doing there?"

"It *is* Tommy Fischer," Violet said. The light in the parking lot lit up enough of the truck so they could see the logo of the jumping fish on the side.

"That's strange," Jessie said. "The visitor center closes at five o'clock."

Just then, the door opened. Ms. Thakur and Tommy came out together. The ranger was carrying a duffel bag, holding it up close to her with both arms. When they reached Tommy's truck, she handed it to him, and he put it inside. Then he drove off, going very fast. Ms. Thakur got in her own car and followed.

Violet didn't want to believe what they'd just seen. "It looks like Ms. Thakur and Tommy Fischer are working together on something," she said. "I just hope it isn't what it looks like."

CHAPTER 9

Seaweed Marks the Spot

The next morning it was still cool and windy. The Aldens walked over to the ranger station. They wanted to pick up some flags in case they saw any more turtle nests on the beach.

"Since we have to leave tomorrow, we should get some postcards too," Jessie said as she headed toward the door of the visitor center.

When she opened it, a gust of wind caught the door and banged it against the wall. Papers from the counter flew up and blew around the room.

"Oh no! I just straightened up the place," Leo said. He came around and began to pick up the papers.

"I'm sorry," said Jessie. "We'll help clean up."

They gathered several items.

The last piece of paper on the floor looked like a handwritten list. Violet picked it up. "This handwriting looks familiar. The letters all have big loops on them."

"That's the ranger's handwriting," Leo said. "It's always so fancy I have trouble reading it sometimes."

The telephone rang. Leo picked it up.

Henry motioned for the others to move away from the counter. "It wasn't Tommy Fischer's handwriting on the sticky note! It was the ranger's!"

"But that means Ms. Thakur was writing to say she knew how *Tommy* could make more money," Jessie said. "Not the other way around."

Just then Ms. Thakur came out of her office carrying a book. It was a bird guide. "Good morning, Aldens," the ranger said as she laid it on the counter. She turned to Leo. "My cousin will be by to pick up this book either today or tomorrow."

Jessie decided it was time to speak up to the ranger about what they'd seen. "We thought we saw you and Tommy Fischer last night," she said. "We were a little worried that something was wrong because it was after the center had closed."

The ranger nodded. "That was us. I gave Tommy some other books about birds, but I forgot about this one. I've been talking to him about adding some bird-watching trips to his business."

"I thought you said this book was for your cousin," said Benny.

"Yes, that's right. Tommy *is* my cousin. I encouraged him to come here and start his fishing business. I didn't know he'd have such a hard time getting it going. I haven't had much a chance to help him since it's nesting season." She looked out the window. "It's another windy day. I need to get out and watch for turtles."

After the ranger left, Jessie picked out some postcards, and the children headed to the beach.

"So Tommy's business *is* having trouble," said Henry. "And he *is* working with Ms. Thakur. But he is going to start bird-watching tours. He's not collecting turtle eggs!"

"I'm so relieved," said Violet. "That's two suspects off our list. Now we just have to catch the real culprit."

"I think I have a way we can figure it out!" Jessie said. "If we see turtles digging, let's mark the real nests with piles of seaweed and shells, so only we know where it is. We'll mark some other spots with flags, so if someone digs there, they won't find any eggs."

"I like that idea!" Benny said. "Junior rangers come up with the best ideas."

The children walked up and down the beach for a long time without seeing any turtles. Finally, Benny spotted some tracks and followed them right up to a dune.

"I'll get some seaweed," Henry said. "We should use enough seaweed and shells so we can be sure to find the nest again."

"Let's count how many steps we take to where we are going to put the flag," Violet said. "That way we'll be extra sure we know where to go."

Jessie suggested fifty steps would be a good amount. They counted as they walked and then placed a flag when they had walked far enough.

"What do we do now?" Benny asked.

"I suppose we keep looking for turtles, but we

also come back here to check on the nest," Henry said.

The Aldens didn't see another turtle until they were much farther up the beach. It was Violet who spotted it. They went through the same process of marking the nest with seaweed and shells and then placing the flag fifty steps away.

"I'm going to call the ranger," Jessie said. "We need to let someone know we've found some nests." She punched in the number, gave the ranger the two different locations, and then hung up. "We're going to meet her up by the first nest," she said.

They walked back down the beach.

"I see Martina," Jessie said. She started to run. The others followed. As they got closer, they saw Sandy sniffing the flag and then walking away. Martina stood watching the dog. She had a foam cooler with her. It was just like the ones the rangers used.

The ranger pulled up next to Martina as the Aldens reached her.

"I can't believe you're stealing the eggs!" Violet

cried. She looked at the cooler and remembered what the ranger had said about the items they threw in the dumpster. "You took a cooler from the ranger station the other night, didn't you?"

Ms. Thakur jumped out of her UTV. "What's happening here?"

Martina looked shocked. "I'm not stealing eggs! I'd never do that." She opened the cooler and tipped it so they could see inside. "Look, it's empty."

"Then why do you have it?" asked Jessie. "And why was Sandy sniffing around the flag?"

Martina looked embarrassed. "I have been training Sandy to sniff out the sea turtle nests. He has a very good nose and loves to dig. I thought it would be a good way to find nests that aren't marked. The only thing was, I needed something that had the scent of the eggs, in order to train him. That's why I took a cooler from the dumpster. I didn't want anyone to know what we were doing until I was sure he could find the nests."

"Is that why you were out at night on the beach with Sandy?" Benny asked. "I saw you."

"That's right," said Martina. "We've been

practicing at night. I didn't want Mr. Chatman to see us. He gets so angry when anyone gets close to a nest."

The ranger looked at the cooler and then at Sandy, who was sniffing around in a different spot. "I have to admit, that is a good idea," she said. "How is Sandy doing?"

"As far as I can tell, he's doing very well, but something strange is happening today." Martina pointed at the flag. "Someone has been putting the flags in the wrong places. Sandy hasn't been interested in those sites at all. He's been sniffing around at what I think are the real nests. For some reason, they are marked with seaweed and a ring of shells instead of a flag. I was about to call you so you could come check and see if I'm right."

"You are right!" Jessie said. "We marked the nests so we could try and catch whoever was stealing the eggs. We still don't know who that is."

"Have you seen anything unusual today?" Ms. Thakur asked Martina.

Martina thought for a moment. "I did notice a white van that stopped and seemed to wait for

Sandy and I to leave, and when we didn't, the van drove away."

"A white van?" asked Henry. "I think I know who we should go see next."

They're Off!

Jessie snapped her fingers. "Mr. Chatman has a white van."

"I can't imagine it would be him," the ranger said. "He cares about the turtles."

"I don't know why he would take the eggs, but it really might be him." Jessie told the ranger about how Mr. Chatman had lied about being on the beach the day the eggs went missing, and about how they had seen someone give a cooler to a woman outside Mr. Chatman's restaurant.

"That is very troubling," said Ms. Thakur. "I should go speak to him, and you all should come along. You kids seem to know what's going on here better than anybody."

They're Off!

The Aldens rode with Ms. Thakur to the Laughing Gull. Martina and Sandy followed in Martina's car.

Outside, Mr. Chatman's white van was in the parking lot, but when the group walked up to the front door, they saw a handwritten sign taped to it, which said *Closed until Wednesday*. There were no lights on.

Martina peered through the glass. "That's strange. I thought they were open every day," she said.

"Let's go around to the back," the ranger suggested. "I want to get to the bottom of this."

Henry knocked on the back entrance.

Mr. Chatman opened the door. "I'm sorry. We're closed today."

"We'd like to talk to you," the ranger said. "It's important."

Mr. Chatman's face turned pale.

Ms. Thakur walked into the kitchen. The others followed. "Mr. Chatman, we think you've been stealing the turtle eggs," the ranger said. She told him the things that Martina and the Aldens had told her.

Mr. Chatman looked ashamed. "I did. I'm sorry. I was only trying to help."

Henry couldn't believe what he was hearing. "How could selling the eggs help the turtles?"

"I didn't sell the eggs!" Mr. Chatman said.

"You just said you took them. And we saw you giving a container to someone who came to the back door last night," Jessie said.

Mr. Chatman took out a handkerchief and wiped his forehead. "That was some extra food in that cooler. I give it to the person who runs a homeless shelter on the mainland. The eggs are all here, safe and sound."

He led the children to a small room full of big coolers.

"I don't understand," the ranger said.

"I want to help the turtles," Mr. Chatman explained. "I took the eggs because your method of trying to save them isn't good enough. There are still too many that don't survive once they reach the water. They're too little. I thought if I raised them in my tank until they were bigger, they might have a better chance of survival."

They're Off!

"No, Mr. Chatman!" The ranger became very upset. "The turtles won't know how to survive in the ocean if they spend time in a tank. And even if they do survive, they may not breed as adults. I thought you knew that. What you are doing is hurting the turtles, not helping them."

Mr. Chatman turned even more pale. Jessie thought he looked like he was going to be sick. "I thought I did know about turtles," he said. "But I guess I still had some things to learn. I was very careful with the eggs. Do you think they'll still hatch?"

Ms. Thakur looked into each container. "Since you haven't had them long, they still have a good chance of survival. But even if they do survive, what you did was very serious. I'm afraid I'm going to have to make a report, and you will have to pay a fine."

Mr. Chatman hung his head. "I understand," he said.

"If you will all help me get these eggs loaded into my car, I'll get to work trying to save them as soon as I get back to the center."

The Sea Turtle Mystery

As soon as all the containers were in Ms. Thakur's car, she got in. "I hope to see the rest of you tomorrow," she said. A faint smile appeared on her face. "We do have one good bit of news. Some turtles at the station are hatching right now. We'll release them bright and early in the morning. Be there at six thirty if you want to watch."

"We'll be there!" Jessie said.

The ranger drove off. Mr. Chatman watched her go. "I'm sorry," he said again. "Everything has gone wrong."

"Why is your restaurant closed, Mr. Chatman?" Jessie asked.

Mr. Chatman looked up at the restaurant building. "I didn't tell Ms. Thakur this, but I thought having sea turtles in the tank would help bring people to the restaurant. After all, they are what the island is known for. I needed to do something to help the restaurant. I can't understand why I don't have more customers."

"Some people think your restaurant is too fancy," Benny blurted.

"They do?" Mr. Chatman sounded surprised. "I

didn't know that. What do you mean?"

"We can show you if we go inside," Violet said. As soon as they were in the dining room, Violet pointed up to the chandeliers. "They are really pretty, but they are also very fancy."

"It's so fancy I feel like I have to whisper in here," Benny said softly.

"I thought having an elegant restaurant would set us apart from the other places to eat around here," Mr. Chatman said.

"But people don't want to come here after being on the beach," Jessie said. "They don't want to feel like they have to get dressed up."

Mr. Chatman went over to the front windows and looked out onto the beach. "Maybe that's why our lunch business is so slow. But I don't know much about decorating. I only know about food. How could I fix it so people would want to come here? What would attract children your age?" he asked Benny and Violet.

"Keep the little boat baskets," Benny said. "I like those!"

"You could make it look like more fun to eat

here," Violet said "It's not very colorful. The fish are colorful, but everything else is just white and gray."

Martina walked around the restaurant.

"The children are right. It doesn't seem like a beach restaurant. I have an idea, a trade, you might call it. I'm an artist. I can help you figure out some new colors and how to change the decorations."

Mr. Chatman held up his hands. "I don't know. I can't pay you very much at all."

"You wouldn't have to pay me much if you'd let me show and sell some of my artwork in your entry area."

"Martina makes shell pictures," Violet said. "The tourists like them."

Mr. Chatman thought for a moment. "I suppose that might work. Why don't you bring some in and let me take a look at them?"

"I have another idea that might help you, and Tommy Fischer too," Henry said.

"Tommy Fischer! Why would I want to help him?" Mr. Chatman frowned.

"He's having a hard time with his business too. The people he takes fishing have to bring their own food. He's not allowed to provide it, but they don't like it when they run out. You could make picnic lunches for people to pick up before they go fishing or before they spend the day on the beach. Tommy could send them here to order."

Mr. Chatman sat down at a table. "You know, that's a very good idea. I could do that. I make some amazing sandwiches, if I do say so for myself."

"What kind?" Benny asked. He realized he was getting very hungry.

"Well, since you are here and the restaurant isn't open, let me make you some. If you like them, I'll add them to the menu."

The sandwiches were very good. When the children were finished, Martina took them back to the beach. The Aldens spent the rest of the afternoon there. In the evening, Grandfather joined them for a final cookout, but they went to bed early so they could wake up for the turtle release.

The next morning the sun had just risen when the Aldens headed for the ranger station.

Park rangers were roping off a narrow strip of sand and putting netting up above it. When the children reached the site, a ranger directed them to a spot behind a rope.

"Hatchlings use the moon or sunlight shining on the water and the white foam of the waves to help them find their way," the ranger said. "White clothing or shoes can confuse them. Those who are wearing white, please move back to stand behind the others."

Benny looked down at his shirt. It was blue, and he was happy he didn't have the move. Henry's shoes were white, so he stood behind Jessie and Violet.

Two park rangers walked into the water. Both were carrying long poles with fake owls on the ends of them.

"The netting and the plastic owls are to keep away the gulls," one of the rangers explained. "They try to dive down to get the turtles and eat them."

Ms. Thakur arrived. A helper set a big box down on the sand. The ranger spoke to the crowd. "The eggs have to incubate for about fifty days, so the turtles we are releasing today were collected a couple of months ago." She opened the lid.

Violet held her breath. She could hardly wait to

see. Ms. Thakur took a hatchling out of the box and set it down in the sand. Then she reached for another. Violet couldn't believe how small the turtles were. Each one was only a little bigger than a quarter. Soon there were dozens of little hatchlings pulling themselves toward the surf.

"They are so cute!" Violet said. Jessie began to take pictures.

"They don't look like the adults," Henry said. "The babies are a lot darker gray."

"Normally, these turtles hatch at night, so being dark gray is an advantage," one of the other rangers said. "They can make their way to the water in the dark, and it's more difficult for the predators to see them."

"Why don't you just carry them to the water?" Benny asked Ms. Thakur. "It's a long way for a little turtle."

"It is hard for them, but it's necessary. Time spent crawling on the beach is important. These turtles do something called imprinting. We don't understand exactly how it works, but somehow crawling on this beach when they hatch does something to the turtles' brains. Years from now, the female sea turtles that may have traveled thousands of miles away from here will return to the same beaches where they hatched and lay their own eggs."

"That's amazing!" Violet said. She and Benny followed the turtles along the roped-off area toward the water.

The first few turtles reached the water. The waves toppled them over and some of the crowd gasped.

"They can't swim!" a girl cried.

"Just watch," the ranger said. The little turtles struggled, but within a very short time, they figured out how to move their flippers in the water and made their way out to sea.

When the last turtle disappeared into the water, the crowd cheered.

Jessie looked out at the water. She imagined the baby turtles swimming on the underwater currents. "It would be fun to be a ranger here," she said to Violet. "I'd like to see the turtles come back year after year."

"Yes," Violet agreed. "When we get home, I'm going to go to the library and check out some books on sea turtles."

The rangers began to take down the netting and the ropes. The crowd moved away.

"Grandfather will be here soon to pick us up," Henry said. "We need to pack."

They said good-bye to Ms. Thakur, then went back to the campsite. Jessie and Henry took down the tent while Benny and Violet gathered up their gear.

"I'm glad you're still here!" a voice called. It was Martina. She hurried toward them, carrying her usual bags and struggling to hold on to Sandy's leash. "Sandy and I wanted to say good-bye."

Violet was happy to see Martina. "I was afraid you'd be angry at us because we thought you and Sandy had been digging up the turtle eggs."

Martina set down the bags. "I understand why you suspected us. I should have just told the ranger what I was trying to do. It's all right though. No harm done."

She reached into one of the bags and took out four little turtles made of seashells. "These are for you, so you can remember Padre Island."

"Thank you!" Jessie said. "This has been such a good trip we won't ever forget it."

"I hope you'll come back sometime," Martina said. "And when you do, maybe you'd like to come on a bird-watching trip with me. Tommy Fischer is doing bird-watching tours now in addition to fishing trips. He's going to hire me to lead some. Between that and selling my shell pictures at The Laughing Gull, Sandy and I should be able to spend plenty of time at the beach."

Jessie got her camera. "Let's get a picture of all of us together, so we have something to remember."

Everyone gathered together for a picture. Jessie held up the camera in front of them. "Say cheese," she said.

"No, say turtle!" Benny said.

"Turtle!"

Turn the page to read a
sneak preview of

THE
HUNDRED-YEAR
MYSTERY

the next
Boxcar Children mystery!

Ghosts, ghosts, ghosts. Will there be ghosts? Six-year-old Benny Alden biked far behind his brother and sisters. Usually he pedaled the fastest, leading the way. Not today. Not where they were going.

Benny could see the others far ahead. Fourteen-year-old Henry was in front. Twelve-year-old Jessie and ten-year-old Violet biked close behind. The curvy bike path led away from Greenfield. The Aldens had never followed this path before. They never had a reason to go this way. Until now.

Will there be ghosts? Benny shivered. He fell farther and farther behind. *Ghosts, ghosts, ghosts.* That's all he'd thought about since breakfast—since what Grandfather had said.

***

This morning at breakfast, Benny had talked and talked and talked about his hundred-day project. Everyone at Benny's school needed to collect one hundred of something, or make one hundred of something, or do one hundred somethings. But Benny couldn't think of one hundred of anything that wasn't boring.

He'd tried a bunch of things. Gluing one hundred pennies on ping-pong paddles? *Bor-ing.* Stringing one hundred pieces of popcorn? *Bor-ing.* Bending one hundred pipe cleaners into animal shapes? *Bor-ing.* His best idea had been to collect one hundred worms. For two days he dug all around the backyard. But he only found ten worms. He set them free.

Then, at breakfast, Grandfather had asked, "How would the four of you like to take a tour of Wintham Manor?"

"Isn't that the giant gray house on the hill?" Jessie asked.

"That's Wintham Manor, all right," said Grandfather. "No one's lived there for a hundred years."

"Why not?" Benny asked.

Grandfather wiggled his eyebrows and said, "That is one of the many mysteries of Wintham Manor. My friend Ella leads tours there and said you're welcome to come. She told me the Manor will be one hundred years old next month." Grandfather smiled at Benny. "With all your talk of one hundred this and one hundred that, I think a hundred-year-old house is a perfect place to visit."

"But," Benny said, "I can't carry a whole house to school for my project."

Grandfather had laughed. "No, I expect not. But Wintham Manor might give you a helpful idea or two. Besides, the four of you have been wanting to bike to someplace you've never been before. Today seems a perfect day for a new adventure."

***

Henry, Jessie, and Violet had all liked Grandfather's suggestion. So now the children were biking to visit the mysterious old house. What bothered Benny was why no one had lived in Wintham Manor for a hundred years. He could think of only one good reason. *Ghosts.* People were afraid to live in Wintham Manor...because it was haunted!

In the distance, Henry and the girls biked up a hill past a group of tall rocks. Benny shuddered.

The rocks looked like giant fingers reaching up out of the ground. A few minutes later he got to the rocks and stopped. They didn't look as scary close up. Benny noticed something strange on the tallest finger. Someone had carved marks near the bottom. The markings were old and worn. They sort of looked like words, but different.

What if it's a warning? Benny wondered. What if it means "danger"? Benny jumped on his bike, pedaling as fast as he could until he caught up with the others.

As the sun moved higher in the sky, the bike path took a sharp curve along a creek. That's when the children saw the manor. The dirty stone building stood like a castle on the next hill. Henry stuck his right arm out and down. It was their signal to stop. The Aldens stared at the giant house. A dark cloud passed over it. Benny's heart thumped as the house fell into the shadow of the cloud.

One corner of Wintham Manor was a huge stone tower. Violet pointed to the top. "Look at that big window," she said. "It's like the tower where Rapunzel let down her hair."

"The whole house looks like something out of a fairy tale," said Jessie.

"Or a scary movie," said Benny, "with ghosts."

"Wintham Manor is not scary," said Jessie. "It's just old."

"How do you know?" Benny asked.

"Because," said Jessie, "Grandfather would never send us anyplace like that."

Henry smiled. "I wouldn't let anything hurt my favorite little brother. Not even some old ghost."

Jessie knew how to move Benny's mind away from ghosts. "I could use some water and a snack before we bike up that hill," she said.

"Me too!" said Benny, opening his backpack. He still wasn't sure about ghosts, but he was sure he was hungry. Benny unwrapped a fig bar and started talking about his hundred-day project...again.

Jessie sighed. "Benny, you're really going to have to choose a project soon." She tore open a small bag of pretzels. "Maybe it won't be perfect, but it has to be *something*."

Benny stuck out his jaw. "It's not my fault I was sick when the hundred-day project started," he said. "By the time I got back to school, all the good ideas were taken." Benny folded the entire cookie into his mouth.

"I tried to give you one hundred buttons," said Jessie, "and Violet offered a hundred colored pencils, and Henry said you could pick out a hundred nails."

"Mgshwidlfhst." Benny tried to speak, but his mouth was too full.

Henry laughed. "What did you say?"

"Benny," whispered Violet, "you should finish chewing before you talk."

Benny chewed and chewed. Then he swallowed. "I want my project to be something really, *really* different," he said finally.

The children ate their snacks in silence. This was going to be one project Benny would have to figure out for himself. When they finished, Jessie collected their garbage into a bag to throw away later. She looked around at the blue creek and the green trees and the big manor on the next hill. It gave her an idea. "If we have time," she said, "I'd like Violet to take a few photos for my blog."

Jessie's blog was called *Where in Greenfield?* Every week she posted a photo of something around town—a tree house, a playground, a statue. Her readers sent in guesses about where in Greenfield the photo was taken. The next week, Jessie blogged the answer and posted a new photo. She thought the creek would be the perfect place for this week's entry.

Henry checked his watch and said, "Okay, let's meet back here in fifteen minutes."

Violet pulled her camera from her bike basket. Jessie took out the notebook and pen she always carried in her pocket. As the girls went exploring, the boys took off their shoes and socks and waded into the creek. A swarm of tadpoles darted away. "I could bring one hundred tadpoles for my project," said Benny.

Henry laughed. "You would have to catch them first." He picked up a flat stone and skipped it across the water. The stone skipped five times. He found another stone for Benny. "Hold it sideways, like this," said Henry. He moved Benny's fingers around the edges. Benny's first stone sank. But after a few tries, Benny could skip a stone two and three times.

For a while, Benny forgot about the project. But when they stopped skipping stones, the thoughts came back. "I'll never have a good idea," he said. "Never, ever, *ever*."

"Sometimes," said Henry, "when I have a problem I can't solve, I just stop thinking about it."

"Huh?" said Benny.

"I know it sounds strange," Henry said. "But when I ignore my problem, I get busy doing other things."

"Like what?" asked Benny.

"Like building that new doghouse for Watch or fixing Grandfather's record player or going for a long run. Pretty soon the answer to my problem sneaks up on me. The more I ignore it, the closer it comes. Then, one day, the answer jumps in front of me and shouts, 'Here I am!'"

Benny thought about this. "So, I should stop worrying about the project?" he asked.

"That's right," said Henry. "Let's go to Wintham Manor to see what a hundred-year-old house looks like. I bet watching out for ghosts makes you forget all about your problem."

Henry lay back on the bank of the creek and closed his eyes. Benny lay back and watched puffy clouds change into different shapes: a dog, a bear, a shoe, a snowman. He liked listening to the sound of water in the creek. He liked feeling the cool ground under him. This place reminded him of when the children lived in the woods.

After their parents died, the Alden children had run away from home. They had been afraid to go and live with their grandfather because they thought he would be mean. The children searched and searched for a place to live. Then one night, they took shelter in an old railroad car in the woods. They decided to make that boxcar their home. They even found a dog named Watch and kept him as their pet. The children had many adventures in the boxcar. They even played in a creek just like this one. Then they met Grandfather, who had been searching for them. He wasn't mean at all! Now the children lived with Grandfather in Greenfield. They used the boxcar as their clubhouse.

Just as Benny was starting to relax, Violet and Jessie came back.

"Time to hit the road," said Henry.

This time Benny kept up with the others. He still wasn't sure he wanted to meet ghosts. But, together, he knew the four of them could face whatever was waiting for them at Wintham Manor.

Introducing The Boxcar Children Early Readers!

Adapted from the beloved chapter books, these new early readers allow kids to begin reading with the stories that started it all. Look for *The Yellow House Mystery* and *Mystery Ranch*, coming Spring 2019!

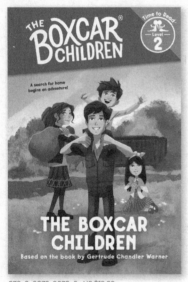

978-0-8075-0839-8 · US $12.99

978-0-8075-7675-5 · US $12.99

978-0-8075-2850-1 · US $6.99

Introducing Interactive Mysteries!

Have you ever wanted to help the Aldens crack a case? Now you can with this interactive, choose-your-path-style mystery!

The Boxcar Children, Fully Illustrated!

This fully illustrated edition celebrates Gertrude Chandler Warner's timeless story. Featuring all-new full-color artwork as well as an afterword about the author, the history of the book, and the Boxcar Children legacy, this volume will be treasured by first-time readers and longtime fans alike.

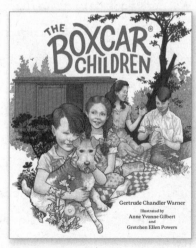

978-0-8075-0925-8 · US $34.99

GERTRUDE CHANDLER WARNER discovered when she was teaching that many readers who like an exciting story could find no books that were both easy and fun to read. She decided to try to meet this need, and her first book, *The Boxcar Children*, quickly proved she had succeeded.

Miss Warner drew on her own experiences to write the mystery. As a child she spent hours watching trains go by on the tracks opposite her family home. She often dreamed about what it would be like to set up housekeeping in a caboose or freight car—the situation the Alden children find themselves in.

While the mystery element is central to each of Miss Warner's books, she never thought of them as strictly juvenile mysteries. She liked to stress the Aldens' independence and resourcefulness and their solid New England devotion to using up and making do. The Aldens go about most of their adventures with as little adult supervision as possible—something else that delights young readers.

Miss Warner lived in Putnam, Connecticut, until her death in 1979. During her lifetime, she received hundreds of letters from girls and boys telling her how much they liked her books.